Tío Armando

Tío Armando

Florence Parry Heide & Roxanne Heide Pierce

illustrated by Ann Grifalconi

Lothrop, Lee & Shepard Books ✧ Morrow
NEW YORK

Watercolor brush and pencil were used for the full-color illustrations.
The text type is 14-point Century 725.

Published by Lothrop, Lee & Shepard Books
an imprint of Morrow Junior Books
a division of William Morrow and Company, Inc.
1350 Avenue of the Americas, New York, NY 10019
http://www.williammorrow.com

Printed in Hong Kong by South China Printing Company (1988) Ltd.

1 2 3 4 5 6 7 8 9 10

Library of Congress Cataloging-in-Publication Data
Heide, Florence Parry.
Tío Armando / by Florence Parry Heide and Roxanne Heide Pierce;
illustrated by Ann Grifalconi.
p. cm.
Summary: When Lucitita's great-uncle Armando comes
to live with them, he teaches her many truths about life.
ISBN 0-688-12107-1 (trade)—ISBN 0-688-12108-X (library)
[1. Family life—Fiction. 2. Great-uncles—Fiction. 3. Death—Fiction.]
I. Pierce, Roxanne Heide. II. Grifalconi, Ann, ill. III. Title. PZ7.H36Tk 1998
[Fic]—dc20 93-37434 CIP AC

To our special friends
the Llanas family
—FPH & RHP

May

Tío Armando has come to live with us. He is the brother of my grandmother, so he is my great-uncle. I call him my uncle, my *tío*.

My grandmother, Abuelita, is wearing black for someone this year. We have a big family. For her, there is always someone to mourn. Tío Armando says that when you have a big family there is always someone to celebrate, someone to be happy about. He is an old man, small. He says he and I have the little bones in the family. Maybe we were meant to be birds, he says.

Since he came, our house is different. Now everything and everyone is joined together. Before, everyone was separate—Mama and Papa; my little brothers, Eduardo and Julio; and the new baby, Rosita. Now, because of Tío Armando, everything that happens seems to happen to all of us.

June

I had not noticed Tío Armando's ring before. It is a silver ring. He made it himself. Thin bands of silver twine and twine together until they seem to be one band. Tío Armando said that this is the way people's lives are, twining together until one life is part of another life, one person is part of another person.

He was making it for Tía Amalia, his wife, but she died before it was ready. He has been wearing it ever since he finished it.

He said that Amalia had taught him a wonderful secret. "I wonder what it is," I said.

But he just smiled at me and said, "Later, *querida*, my dear one, another time." So I don't know what the secret is.

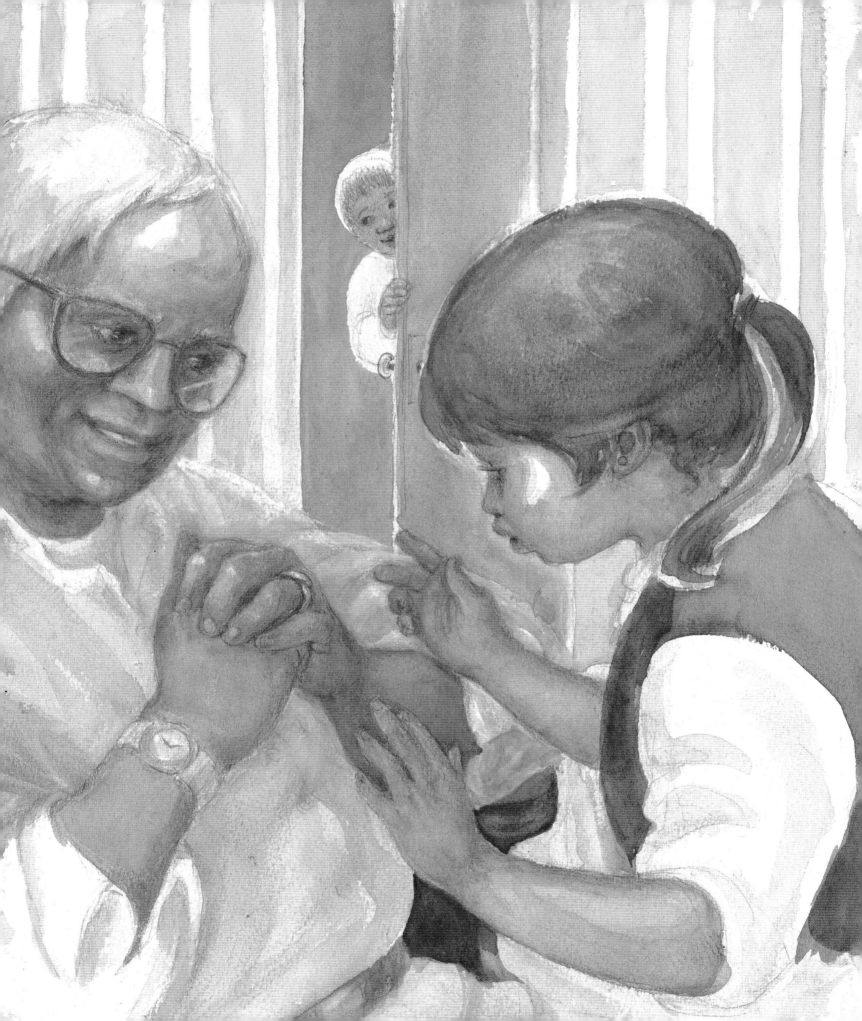

July

I wanted to talk to Tío Armando about our visits together.
He laughed and said, "A talk about talking!"

What I wanted to say was that he and I talk mostly about
ideas. Mama and Papa and Abuelita talk always about
definite things: about food or how much things cost and
where you can get something cheaper.

Tío Armando chuckled. "But that's the way life must be,
Lucitita. *Someone* must take care of all that. But you and I,
how lucky we are! You to be young, I to be old! You can
look ahead. I can look back."

"You'll never go away, will
you?" I asked.

He looked at me. "I will
never leave you," he said.

August

Mama asked me to go to the hospital to find Tío Armando and to ask him to come home early for supper. Tío Armando likes to go to the hospital. He sits in the lobby and looks at the papers and the magazines. Sometimes he stays with the children who wait there while their mamas and papas visit someone who is sick.

If you want to see a patient, the lady at a desk in the lobby gives you a card. Then you can take the elevator upstairs to see your sick friend. But Tío Armando has no one sick now, so he listens for names that other people say, and then later he tells that name to the lady at the desk. That way he can get a visitor's card. Always he takes a little present: a flower or a packet of seeds or a magazine.

I said, "But they don't know you. You don't know them."

He said, "It doesn't matter. They know that someone brought a present. That is enough. I do not myself go in to see them. The nurse takes it in later. She says it is from a friend."

September

Last night I gave Rosita her bottle and tucked her in her crib. When it was time for the boys to go to bed, Julio cried. He is afraid of the dark.

Tío Armando went in to comfort him. "This is exactly the same room at night as it is in the daytime," he said. "The only difference is that the light has gone to sleep. And when you wake up tomorrow, the light will already be up, waiting."

Then Julio said, "Tell us a story, Tío. Tell us a story."

Tío Armando told them about how he had met Amalia at a fiesta, and about the time they got on a bus and just rode until they saw a pretty place to stop. "And we stayed there forever," he said.

Julio said, "That isn't a story!"

Tío laughed. He asked, "What is a story, Julio?"

Eduardo said, "A story has an ending!"

Then Julio shouted, "A story is made up!"

"Some stories have endings," Tío Armando said. "And some stories keep going forever. Some stories are made up, and some are real."

Later I heard Julio giggling with Eduardo. He was not afraid of the dark when he went to sleep.

October

Ever since he came to live with us, Tío Armando has spent a part of every day in the library. Saturday I walked there with him. He goes the same way each time, passing the same houses and streets and stores and people every day. People waved to him and smiled.

It was the same in the library. The librarians knew him, and in the reading room, people looked up and smiled when he came in. "How do you understand each other when you speak only Spanish, and most of your friends speak only English?" I asked.

"Friends can talk without talking," Tío Armando said.

One of the old men is poor. Each day he comes to the library. He cannot read, but he looks at the magazines and stays warm. Tío Armando brings fruit and sandwiches, pretending that it is his own lunch and that he cannot finish. The old man takes the food home with him.

As we walked back home on Saturday, Tío Armando said, "If I didn't go one day, would anyone notice? Would they feel a difference in their days?"

Lately he turns and turns his silver ring around and around on his finger.

November

Mama and Abuelita are teaching me to cook. Already
I can make frijoles and chicken mole and Spanish rice, and
last week I made the whole supper for our family, with
guacamole and enchiladas. Everyone said it was as good as
Mama's or Abuelita's.

Tío Armando asked me if I could prepare a banquet for
his friends. We planned the menu. He will invite the old man
at the library. And he is going to ask some of the friends he
sees on his walks, and someone he met in the hospital. We
are planning it for next summer, so that they can sit out in
the yard after dinner.

December

Eduardo cried today because there was no snow for a
snowman. He said, "You promised we could make snowmen!"
He is such a baby.

"It can't be helped," said Tío Armando. "The snow
didn't last."

Eduardo kept whining. "Nothing lasts!"

Tío Armando looked at me. "Love lasts," he said. Then he
called us all out into the kitchen, Julio and Eduardo and me.
We sat around the kitchen table and made snowmen out of
toothpicks and marshmallows. We had pieces of raisins for
the eyes, and we unraveled an old red sweater of Julio's to
make scarves for our snowmen.

Then Tío Armando and I made popcorn. He said to
Eduardo, "You see, there is never a reason to cry about
something like that. A promise is not broken. It comes true in
a different way at a different time—that is all."

Eduardo took his marshmallow snowman to bed with him.